CW00853698

AFRICAN STORIES

For Edis — K W-M

To Patricia. Like an elephant, we'll never forget you — S.B.

HODDER CHILDREN'S BOOKS
First published in Great Britain in 2024 by
Hodder & Stoughton

3 5 7 9 10 8 6 4 2

A CIP catalogue record for this book
is available from the British Library.

PB ISBN 9781 444 97500 0
E-book ISBN 978 1444 97501 7

Printed in China
Hodder Children's Books
An imprint of Hachette Children's Group
Part of Hodder & Stoughton Limited
Carmelite House
50 Victoria Embankment
London, EC4Y 0DZ

An Hachette UK Company
www.hachette.co.uk
www.hachettechildrens.co.uk

Once Upon an ELEPHANT

Ken Wilson-Max

Subi Bosa

Sometimes, out in the thick bush, you might hear leaves rustling or twigs breaking. You might even see branches moving when there is no wind.

If you keep very still,
you will probably see . . .

. . . a BIG elephant with large flappy ears, long white tusks, and an even longer trunk!

TERRRUMPET!

But, once upon a time, Elephant looked very different. He had a short, stumpy nose.

As noses go, Elephant's worked quite well, and it never got in the way.

But he couldn't reach the fruit in the tall trees . . .

. . . and it took him AGES to wash his back!

One day, Elephant kneeled down to drink from the watering hole. He dipped his short, stubby nose in the water, just a little bit.

But it was enough for sneaky . . .

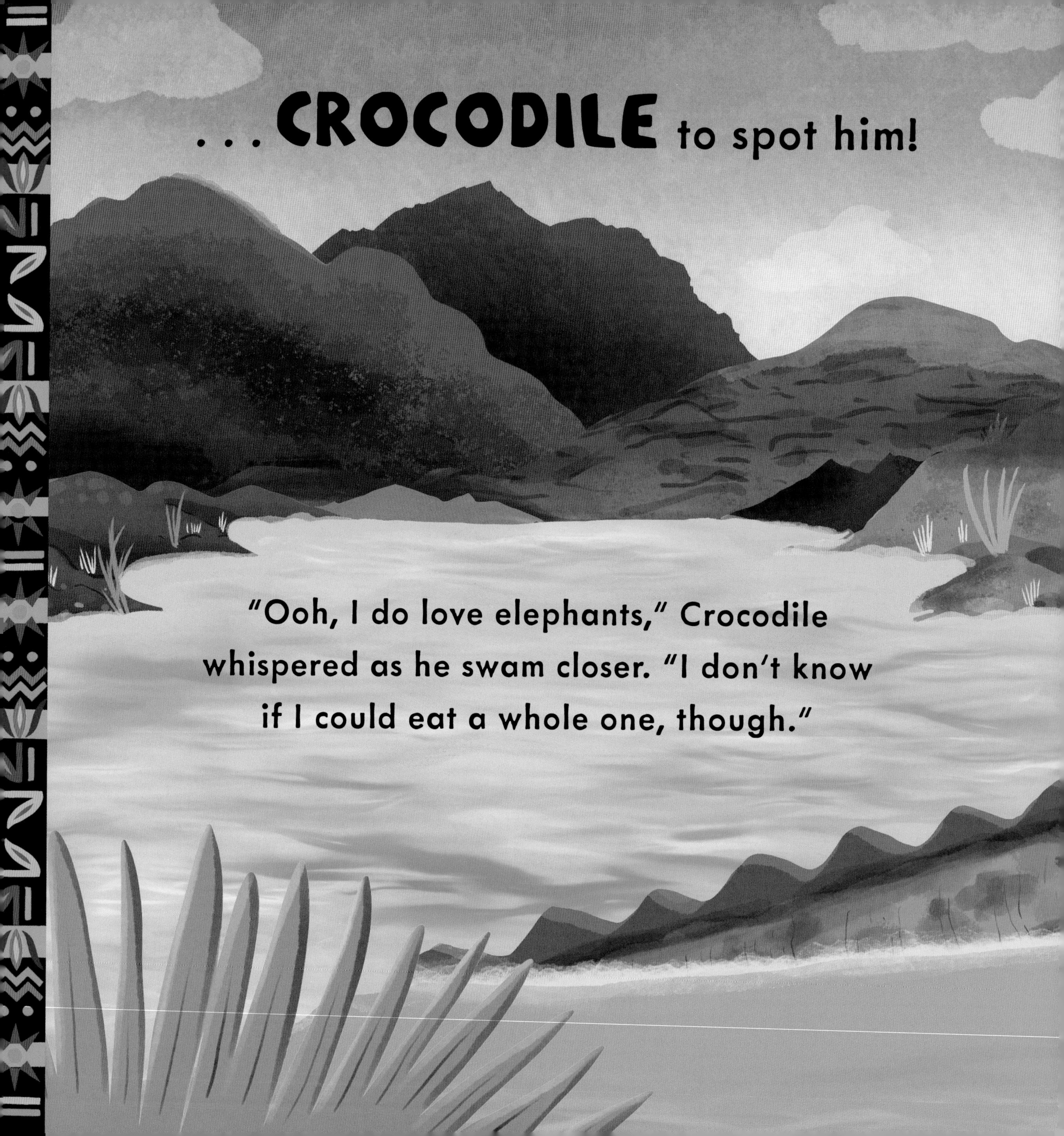

. . . **CROCODILE** to spot him!

"Ooh, I do love elephants," Crocodile whispered as he swam closer. "I don't know if I could eat a whole one, though."

The hungry crocodile saw
his chance and . . .

. . . he grabbed
Elephant's nose!

SNAP!

Elephant was strong, and he dug his feet into the mud, but the greedy crocodile was pulling him into the water!

HELLPPPPPP

PP!

The other animals rushed to help Elephant.

"Start pulling!" cried Zebra.

The animals tugged with all their might. And with every pull . . .

Elephant's nose got longer . . .

and longer . . .

and longer
until . . .

...PING!

At last, Crocodile let go and all the animals landed in a big heap!

Crocodile was too tired
to pull any more, and slunk
back under the water.
"Maybe I'll have fish today,"
he sighed.

"OH NO!"
cried Elephant.
"Look at my nose!

All the other elephants
will laugh at me.
What am I going to do?"

But, to his surprise, Elephant found his new nose useful! He could now pick fruit from the tall trees . . .

drink easily from the watering hole . . .

. . . and even take a lovely, big shower
with his new, long nose.

Ever since that day, elephants always win at tug-of-war with their lovely, long noses, while crocodiles stay hungry!

And that is the story
of how elephants got their
LONG trunks!